SHIPWRECKED!

A John M. Jacobsen Production
A Nils Gaup Film

Executive Producer Nigel Wooll

Based upon the book "Haakon Haakonsen" by O.V. Falck-Ytter

Screenplay by
Nils Gaup & Greg Dinner & Bob Foss and Nick Thiel

Produced by John M. Jacobsen
Directed by Nils Gaup

Soundtrack available on cassette and compact disc from Walt Disney Records

Distributed by Buena Vista Pictures Distribution, Inc.
© Buena Vista Pictures Distribution, Inc.

Based on the Walt Disney Picture

Adapted by
William Rotsler

Illustrated by
Dan Spiegle

Lettered by
Carrie Spiegle

Colored by
Carl Gafford

Edited by
David Cody Weiss

Publisher ××××××××××××××××××××××××××××××××× **Randy Achee**

Editor-in-Chief ×××××××××××××××××××××××××××××× **Len Wein**

Managing Editor ×××××××××××××××××××××××××× **Bob Foster**

Production Manager ××××××××××××××××× **Barbara Pietuch**

Marketing Manager ×××××××××××× **Sally Prendergast**

National Sales Manager ×××××××××××××× **Andrea Beam**

Account Executive for Marketing ××××××××××× **Teri Sokol**

Account Executive for Sales ××××××××××× **Leslie Villegas**

Publishing Co-ordinator ××××××××××××××× **Ellen Stuart**

Production
Cris Palomino

Carl Gafford   Lynn Williams   Arlene Nilsson

IN A PUB NEAR THE LONDON DOCKS...
MORE WINE!

YES, DRINK UP, YOU FOOL!

I KNOW THAT MAN FROM SOMEWHERE--!

KN2690

CHANDLER SHIPPING
IT IS YOU, MERRICK... IN LONDON!
AND IT'S YOU, HOWELL... IN A PREDICAMENT.

BLAM
UH--!

WHAT IS IT NOW, MERRICK? HAVE YOU TAKEN YOUR PIRACY TO THE STREETS?
WHATEVER PAYS...
I HEAR YOU'VE BEEN COMMISSIONED TO A MERCHANT SHIP BOUND FOR AUSTRALIA AND INDIA.

I'LL BE TAKING YOUR SAILING ORDERS.
MY SAILING ORDERS?
YOU'LL NEVER GET AWAY WITH THIS!

OH, WOULDN'T YOU LIKE TO BE THERE TO SEE IT.
A PIRATE CAPTAIN-- WELCOMED ABOARD A MERCHANT SHIP.

BUT THERE CAN ONLY BE ONE OF YA-- AND IT'S GONNA BE ME.

BLAM
NOTING SHIPP

5

NO! NO!
PLEASE!

YOU WAIT
UNTIL MY FATHER
COMES HOME! HE'LL
TAKE CARE OF
ALL OF YOU!

YOU'RE
FATHER ISN'T
COMING HOME!
HE'S LOST AT
SEA!

IF PAPA
WERE ONLY
HERE...
PAPA?
PAPA?
PAPA?

PAPA, I THOUGHT... THAT YOU MIGHT NOT COME HOME!
I PROMISED YOU I WOULD, DIDN'T I?
I WOULDN'T HAVE MADE IT IF IT WASN'T FOR JENS HERE.
I CAUGHT MY LEG IN A LINE AND JENS CUT ME FREE BEFORE I DROWNED.
I HAVE SOMETHING FOR YOU, HAWKON--SOMETHING I DREAMED ABOUT WHEN I WAS YOUR AGE.
A COMMISSION, SON, ON MY SHIP, THE FLORA.
NILS, HE'S...HE'S SO YOUNG!
YOU'RE READY, AREN'T YOU, SON?
SURE, HAWKON'S READY-- AS READY A SAILOR AS I WAS AT HIS AGE. BUT HE CAN'T POSSIBLY GO NOW!
I CAN'T?
JENS IS RIGHT. I CAN'T AFFORD TO LET YOU GO. I'M SORRY, HAWKON.
I CAN WAIT, PAPA.
HOW DO YOU THINK YOU'RE GOING TO BE ABLE TO WORK THE FARM WITH THAT LEG? NO, YOU NEED HAWKON HERE TO HELP WITH THE SPRING PLANTING.

7

THE NEXT MORNING...
I MUST SEE IF MR. WERNES CAN EXTEND OUR LOAN.

I'M SORRY ABOUT YOUR LEG, BUT I HAVE EXPENSES, TOO.
WHEN YOU WERE AT SEA, EARNING A GOOD WAGE, I DIDN'T MIND, BUT NOW...
I'LL PAY YOU BACK AS SOON AS I CAN...

I KNOW YOU'LL TRY... AND I'M NOT THE KIND OF MAN THAT ENJOYS TAKING ANOTHER MAN'S LAND...
I'LL GIVE YOU A FEW WEEKS, BUT THAT'S ALL!
I'LL DO MY BEST.

THAT EVENING...
EVERYONE'S HURTING THIS YEAR, MAGGIE, THEY CAN'T HELP.
EVEN IF WERNES WAITED UNTIL WE HARVESTED, IT WOULDN'T PAY THE WHOLE DEBT.

IF ONLY HAWKON WAS OLDER... IF ONLY HE WANTED TO GO TO SEA.
DON'T WORRY, I'D NEVER SEND HIM UNTIL HE WANTED TO GO.

BUT ONE MONTH LATER...
I'M SORRY ABOUT THIS, NILS.
STRICTLY BUSINESS, HAWKONSEN.
THIS IS OUR FARM NOW. YOU HAVE TO GET OFF. TOMORROW!
BUT THIS IS OUR HOME!
I HATE THIS PART OF THE JOB, BUT IF YOU CAN'T PAY YOUR DEBT...
I'M PAYING THE DEBT.
I'M GOING TO SEA--AS SHIP'S BOY--ON THE FLORA.
ARE YOU SURE, HAWKON?
YES, SIR!
THEY DON'T PAY A SHIP'S BOY WHAT THEY PAY AN EXPERIENCED SAILOR...
HE'LL BE PAID HALF MY WAGES.
THEN HE'LL HAVE TO WORK TWO YEARS TO PAY THE DEBT.
AGREED!

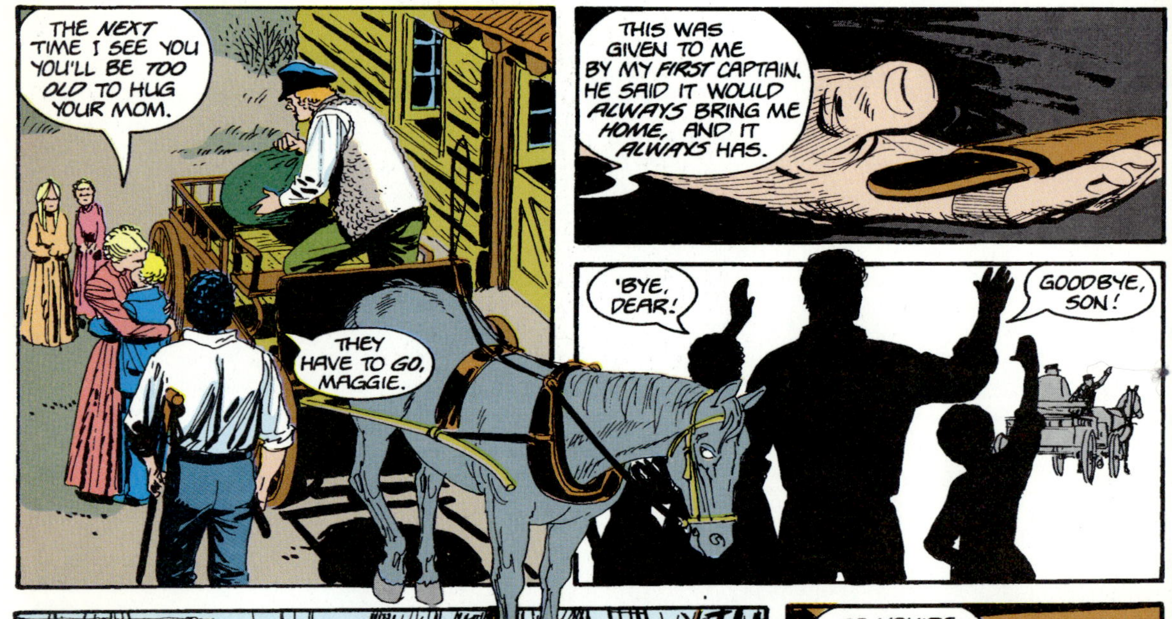

THE NEXT TIME I SEE YOU YOU'LL BE TOO OLD TO HUG YOUR MOM.
THEY HAVE TO GO, MAGGIE.
THIS WAS GIVEN TO ME BY MY FIRST CAPTAIN. HE SAID IT WOULD ALWAYS BRING ME HOME, AND IT ALWAYS HAS.
'BYE, DEAR!
GOODBYE, SON!

LATER, AT THE SEAPORT...
CAPTAIN MADSEN'S CABIN'S THAT WAY. GO AND REPORT.
YES, SIR.

SO YOU'RE NILS' SON, THE NEW SHIP'S BOY.
YES, SIR!

YOU'RE KIND OF PUNY, AREN'T YOU?
WELL, THERE'S NO ROOM ABOARD FOR CHILDREN. YOU WILL WORK HARD, AND YOU'LL BE A SAILOR!
Y-YES, S-SIR!

AWAY ALL LINES!

THE VOYAGE BEGINS.

10

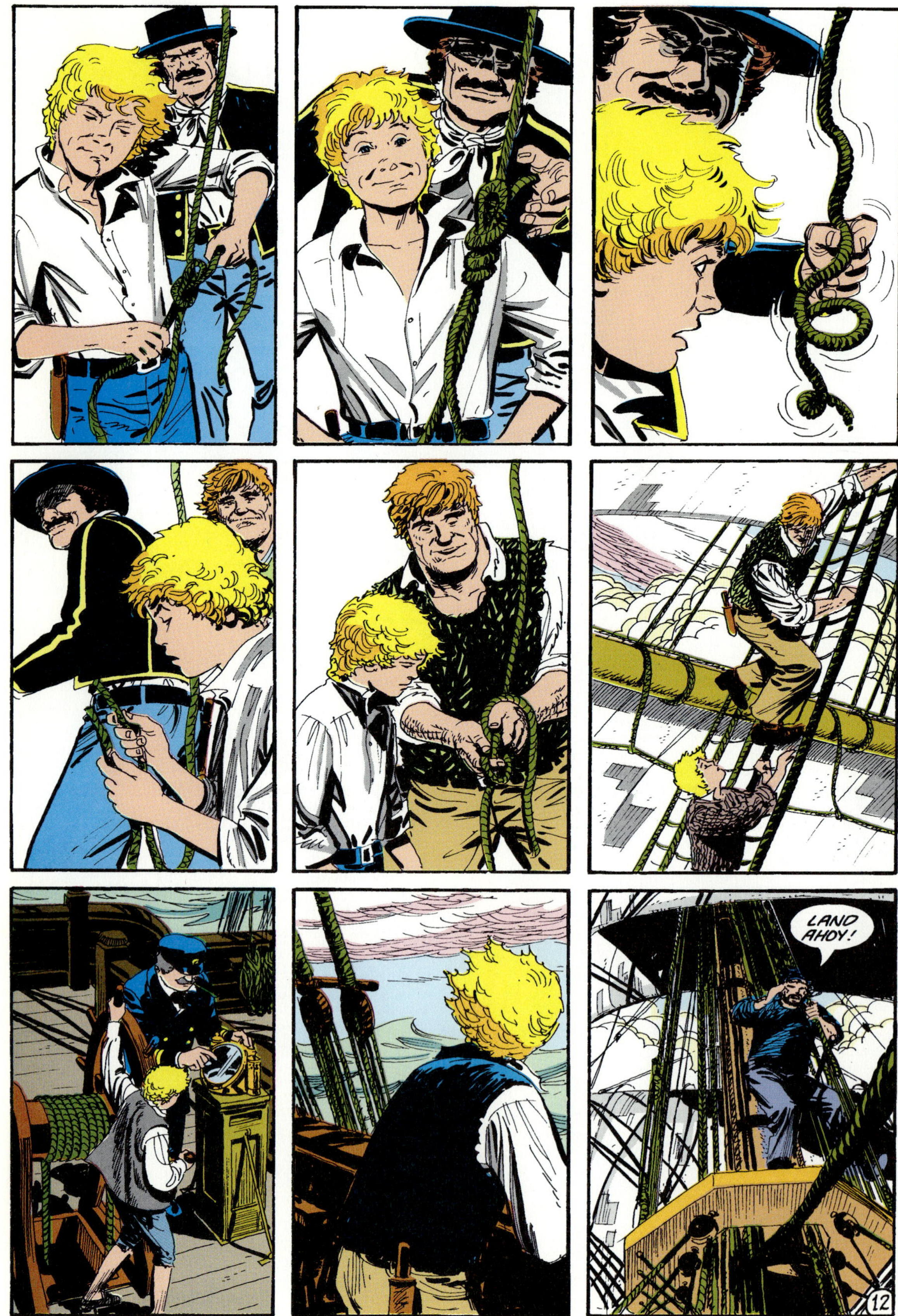
LAND AHOY!

LONDON, ENGLAND... BUSIEST PORT OF THE WORLD'S GREATEST MARITIME NATION...
KEEP A CLOSE WATCH ON YOUR VALUABLES, LAD.

THE SEA BETWEEN SYDNEY AND CALCUTTA IS INFESTED WITH PIRATES. WE'LL EARN OUR PAY THERE.
BRING ON THE PIRATE SCUM! JENS HAS BEEN SHOWING ME HOW TO FIGHT WITH MY SABER!
HO! THOSE PIRATES ARE DONE FOR, THEN!

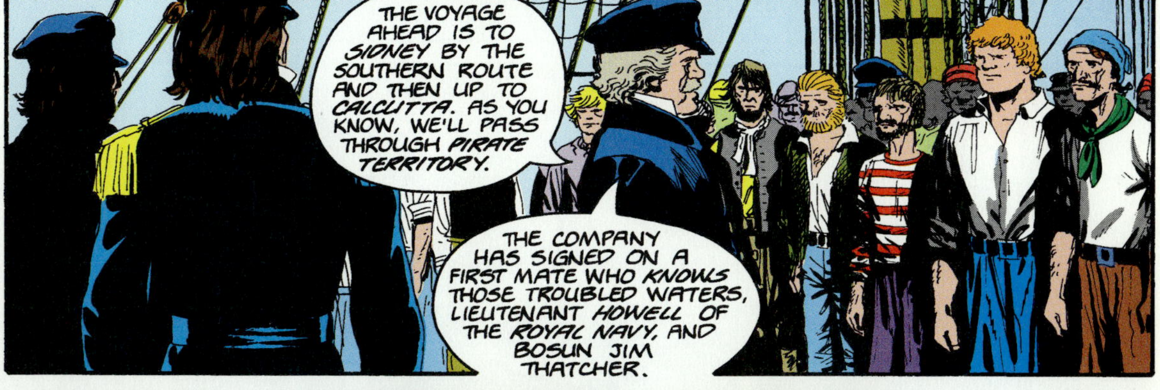

THE VOYAGE AHEAD IS TO SIDNEY BY THE SOUTHERN ROUTE AND THEN UP TO CALCUTTA. AS YOU KNOW, WE'LL PASS THROUGH PIRATE TERRITORY.
THE COMPANY HAS SIGNED ON A FIRST MATE WHO KNOWS THOSE TROUBLED WATERS, LIEUTENANT HOWELL OF THE ROYAL NAVY, AND BOSUN JIM THATCHER.

MISTER HOWELL IS A RESPECTED OFFICER IN THE ROYAL NAVY. HE SAW ACTION WHEN THE PIRATES WERE BOOTED OUT OF BORNEO.
WISH HIM WELCOME!
MISTER HOWELL?

AS A LITTLE INCENTIVE, THE COMPANY HAS AUTHORIZED ME TO PAY A BONUS TO EVERY MEMBER OF THE CREW...IF WE GET TO CALCUTTA AHEAD OF SCHEDULE!
13

THE WEEKS PASS. THE ATLANTIC OCEAN GIVES WAY TO THE INDIAN OCEAN, THEN THE *FLORA* HEADS INTO THE SOUTH PACIFIC.

MISTER THATCHER?
WHAT DO YOU WANT, BOY?
MISTER HOWELL SENT ME TO FIND YOU. HE WANTS HIS *CHARTS*. HE SAID THEY WERE IN A POUCH.

FIND THE POUCH YOURSELF AND BE QUICK ABOUT IT!
YESSIR.

THERE, THAT MUST BE IT.
LT. HOWEL PRIVATE
LT. HOWEL PRIVATE
LT. HOWEL PRIVATE

OH--!
CRASH
LT. HO PRIV

ARE YOU STILL DOWN HERE, BOY?
HU-HERE, SIR!

I FOUND THE POUCH, SIR.
AND MORE, I SEE.

IF THERE'S A SECRET TO BE KEPT, FOR THE GOOD OF THE SHIP AND HER CREW...WELL, ANY GOOD SAILOR KNOWS HOW TO KEEP HIS MOUTH SHUT.
ISN'T THAT RIGHT, YOUNG HAWKON?
I DON'T HAVE ANY SECRETS, S-SIR.

I HEARD A TALE ONCE OF A SAILOR WHO TOLD SOMETHING HE SHOULDN'T HAVE... AND HALF THE CREW WAS LOST.
THE HALF THAT SURVIVED CUT THE SAILOR'S TONGUE OUT AND RAN IT UP THE MAIN HALYARD!
YOU UNDERSTAND WHAT I'M SAYING, BOY?
Y-YES, S-SIR!
SECURE THAT LINE! LOWER THE MAIN SAIL!
STORM BOTHERING YOU, KID?
STORM? WHAT STORM?

...ZZZZ...

THE FOLLOWING AFTERNOON...

I JUST DON'T TRUST MISTER HOWELL, CAPTAIN.

YOU'VE NEVER TRUSTED THE ENGLISH.

I'VE MET LOTS OF BRITISH OFFICERS, SIR. SAY WHAT YOU WILL OF THEM, THEY'RE GENTLEMEN. THIS FELLOW HASN'T THE MANNERS OF A STABLEBOY! YOU'VE SEEN THE WAY HE EATS!

HE'S A DAMN GOOD SAILOR.

IF YOU ASK ME, THERE'S SOMETHING NOT RIGHT ABOUT THIS BRITISH LIEUTENANT HOWELL, SIR. I SAY HE'S TROUBLE.

I'LL BE OVER THIS FEVER IN A DAY OR SO...
IT CAME ON SUDDEN, SIR--YOU BETTER REST.

BUT I HAVE TO TALK TO HIM!
HE NEEDS HIS REST, LAD.

HOW IS THE CAPTAIN?
HIS TEMPERATURE IS HIGH.

THEN IT'S SHIP FEVER?
MOST LIKELY, SIR, BUT I'VE NEVER SEEN SHIP FEVER ATTACK JUST ONE MAN.

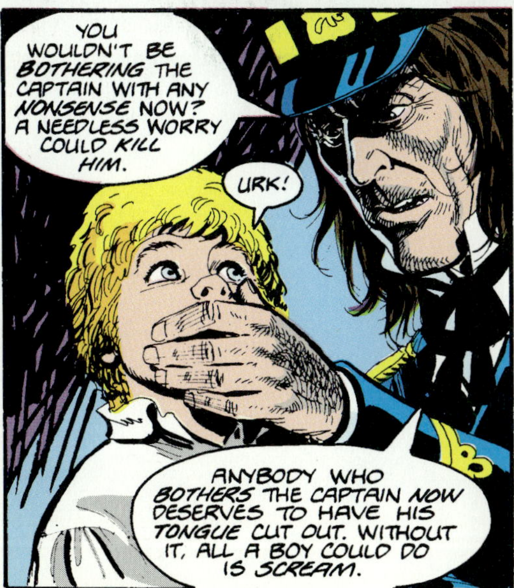

YOU WOULDN'T BE BOTHERING THE CAPTAIN WITH ANY NONSENSE NOW? A NEEDLESS WORRY COULD KILL HIM.
URK!
ANYBODY WHO BOTHERS THE CAPTAIN NOW DESERVES TO HAVE HIS TONGUE CUT OUT. WITHOUT IT, ALL A BOY COULD DO IS SCREAM.

CAPTAIN MORGAN EILIFF MADSEN, WE COMMIT YOUR REMAINS TO THEIR FINAL RESTING PLACE. MAY GOD HAVE MERCY ON YOUR SOUL.

17

HAWKON CONTINUES TO LEARN AS THE FLORA SAILS TOWARD SIDNEY.
GOOD LAD!
ALL HANDS ON DECK!
WE LAND AT SIDNEY TOMORROW, BUT AS WE'RE A DAY BEHIND SCHEDULE, THERE WILL BE NO SHORE LEAVE.
BEGGIN' YOUR PARDON, SIR, BUT WE'RE A DAY AHEAD OF SCHEDULE AND THE CREW'S WORKED HARD FOR THAT SHORE LEAVE!
YOU DARE TO TALK BACK TO AN OFFICER? THIS SHIP IS NOW UNDER THE COMMAND OF THE BRITISH ROYAL NAVY...
...AND WE HANG MEN WHO TALK OF MUTINY!
18

BUT, SIR, I WASN'T--
THEN KEEP YOUR MOUTH SHUT AND DO AS YOU'RE TOLD!
ANYONE ELSE OBJECT TO SACRIFICING SHORE LEAVE FOR THE GOOD OF THE VOYAGE?

THEN GET BACK TO WORK!

THE HARBOR OF THE NEW COLONY OF SIDNEY, IN AUSTRALIA.

LOOK LIVELY NOW!

19

AFTER SEVERAL WEEKS, HAWKON IS STILL UNEASY ABOUT KEEPING THE SECRET OF THE RIFLES.
COULD I SHOW YOU SOMETHING, JENS?
THERE COULD BE PLENTY OF EXPLANATIONS FOR THIS CARGO.
LIKE WHAT?
SOME EXTRA FIREPOWER TO USE AGAINST PIRATES.
HOWELL IS A BRITISH NAVAL OFFICER, HAWKON, AND HE'S CAPTAIN NOW. IT'S HIS BUSINESS, NOW.
WE HAVE TO OBEY THE RULES OF THE SEA-- OR IT'S MUTINY AND WE COULD BE HANGED!
I'LL SHOW YOU WHICH OF THE CAPTAIN'S PRIVATE BOXES TO UNLOAD. THE REST STAY UNTIL WE GET TO ROCK ISLAND.
ROCK ISLAND? WE'RE SUPPOSED TO GO TO CALCUTTA NEXT!
ROCK ISLAND IS IN THE WORST PIRATE WATERS! TAKING A MERCHANT SHIP THERE IS JUST ASKING FOR TROUBLE!
20

THESE ARE YOUR NEW MATES, BOSUN.
YOU DIDN'T SAY ANYTHING ABOUT TAKING ON EXTRA CREW, SIR.
WELL, I'M SAYING IT NOW! I CAN'T TRUST THE LOT OF YOU TO SAIL THIS SHIP ON SCHEDULE!
THE FLORA SAILED NORTH, TO ROUND AUSTRALIA.
SKEEP
COME OUT, WHOEVER YOU ARE!
IS SOMEONE HERE?

MURP!

21

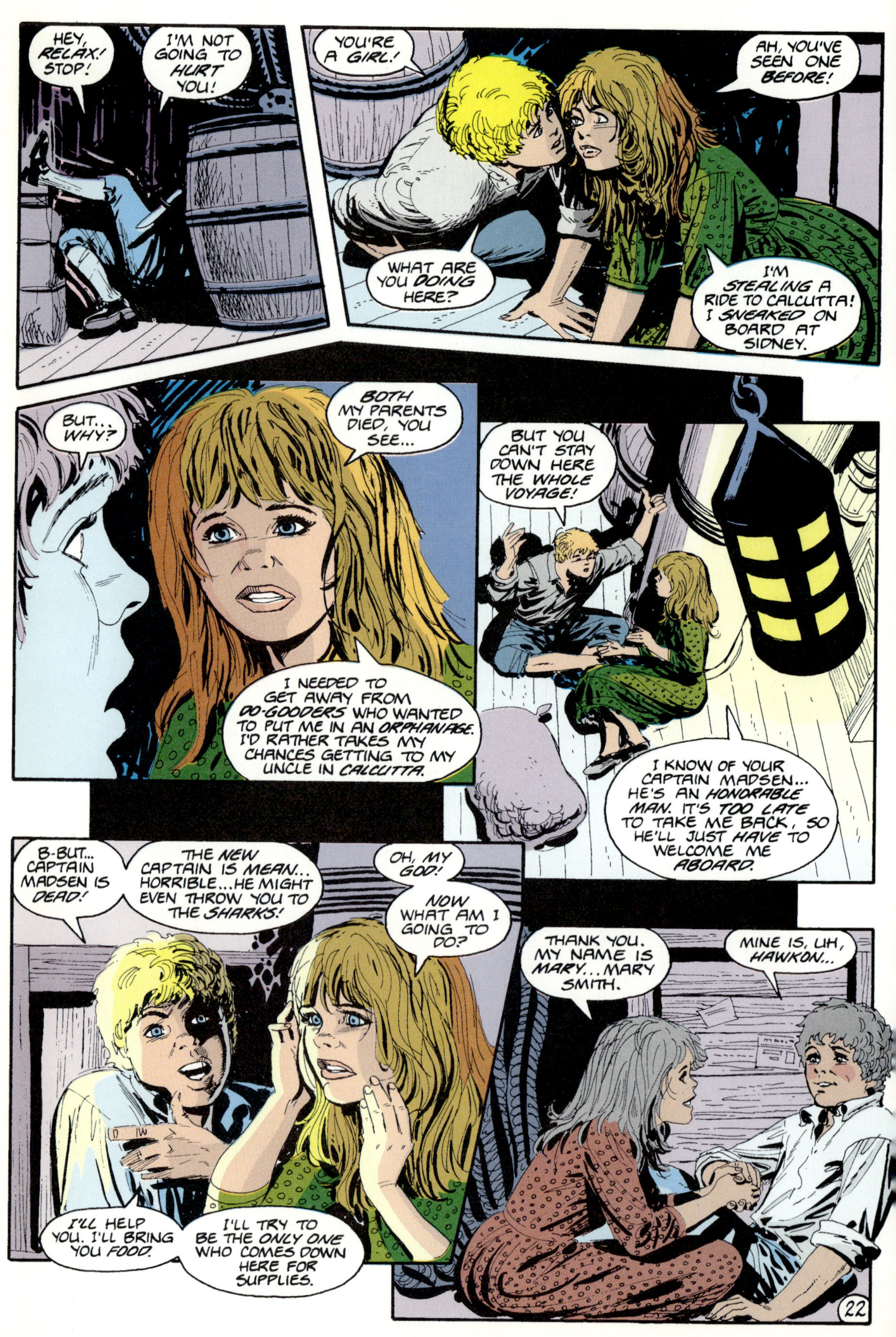

HEY, RELAX! STOP!
I'M NOT GOING TO HURT YOU!
YOU'RE A GIRL!
AH, YOU'VE SEEN ONE BEFORE!
WHAT ARE YOU DOING HERE?
I'M STEALING A RIDE TO CALCUTTA! I SNEAKED ON BOARD AT SIDNEY.
BUT... WHY?
BOTH MY PARENTS DIED, YOU SEE...
I NEEDED TO GET AWAY FROM DO-GOODERS WHO WANTED TO PUT ME IN AN ORPHANAGE. I'D RATHER TAKES MY CHANCES GETTING TO MY UNCLE IN CALCUTTA.
BUT YOU CAN'T STAY DOWN HERE THE WHOLE VOYAGE!
I KNOW OF YOUR CAPTAIN MADSEN... HE'S AN HONORABLE MAN. IT'S TOO LATE TO TAKE ME BACK, SO HE'LL JUST HAVE TO WELCOME ME ABOARD.
B-BUT... CAPTAIN MADSEN IS DEAD!
THE NEW CAPTAIN IS MEAN... HORRIBLE... HE MIGHT EVEN THROW YOU TO THE SHARKS!
OH, MY GOD!
NOW WHAT AM I GOING TO DO?
I'LL HELP YOU. I'LL BRING YOU FOOD.
I'LL TRY TO BE THE ONLY ONE WHO COMES DOWN HERE FOR SUPPLIES.
THANK YOU. MY NAME IS MARY... MARY SMITH.
MINE IS, UH, HAWKON...
22

HEY!
SHUTYA-MOUTH!
THE VOYAGE PROCEEDS, BUT THE NEW SAILORS ARE ARROGANT.
MORE!
OWW--!
WHAT'S THAT?
I DON'T SEE NOTHIN', BOY.
BEAT THAT, YE BLOCKHEAD!

EASY EASY...
WE'LL SLEEP ON THE DECK TONIGHT...
OH! IT'S YOU!
I BROUGHT YOU AN APPLE.
I'LL TRY TO GET MORE FOOD TOMORROW. JUST STAY QUIET UNTIL THEN.
MARY, UH, COULD YOU, UM, TEACH ME TO READ?
I SUPPOSE I COULD...
THE WEATHER WAS BECOMING TROPICAL.

THE WINDS CARRY THE FLORA TOWARD HER DESTINY.

"IN XANADU DID KUBLA KHAN A STATELY PLEASE ...SUR..."
"PLEASURE."

?
NOBODY SAID THE ENGLISH LANGUGE MADE ANY SENSE!

"...STATELY PLEASURE DOME DECREE."
GOOD!

WHAT'S "XANADU"?
MY MOTHER SAID IT WAS THE MOST BEAUTIFUL PLACE ON EARTH, WHERE EVERYBODY WAS HAPPY AND SAFE.

IT DOESN'T REALLY EXIST...
YES, IT DOES...

SO THIS IS WHERE YOU'VE BEEN SNEAKING OFF TO EVERY NIGHT!
IT'S ALL RIGHT, MARY! HE'S JENS, MY FRIEND.

A STOWAWAY, HUH? TOO LATE, OF COURSE, TO TELL YOU HOW FOOLISH THIS IS.
SHE'S AN ORPHAN. SHE HAS TO GET TO A RELATIVE IN CALCUTTA.

25

WELL, NOTHING I CAN SAY ABOUT IT NOW.
OH, HERE'S SOMETHING I FOUND LYING AROUND.
HE WON'T TELL, WILL HE?
I TRUST HIM WITH MY LIFE.

A DAY LATER.
JENS, YOU EVER KISS A GIRL?
A FEW... AND BELIEVE IT OR NOT, SOME OF THEM KISSED ME BACK! ...AND LIKED IT!

ALL HANDS ON DECK!
LINE THE MEN UP FOR INSPECTION!
INSPECTION? BUT—WE NEED EVERY HAND IN THIS STORM!

INSPECTION, YOU INSOLENT DOG! NOW!
WE HAVE HERE A STOWAWAY! ONE OF YOU HAS BEEN HIDING HER AND STEALING FOOD FROM OUR MOUTHS FOR HER!
NOW, MISS, POINT OUT YOUR CONFEDERATE!

WELL...?
AYE, YOU'RE A BRAVE GAL. PITY YOU'VE CHOSEN A COWARD FOR YOUR PROTECTOR.
YOU LEAVE ME NO CHOICE...
BOSUN, PREPARE TO KEELHAUL THE PRISONER!
YOU CAN'T! SHE'S ONLY A CHILD! DRAGGING HER UNDER THE HULL WILL KILL HER!
SO IT WAS YOU, JENS.
TAKE HER AWAY AND PUT HER IN IRONS!
YOU KNOW THE PENALTY FOR HIDING A STOWAWAY!
FETCH ME THE CAT O'NINE TAILS!
NO, WAIT--!
JENS DIDN'T DO ANYTHING --IT WAS ME!
HAWKON!
HOLD YOUR TONGUE! YOUNG MISTER HAWKONSEN WILL TAKE HIS FORTY LASHES LIKE ANY OTHER MAN ON THIS SHIP!
BEGIN!

THAT WHIP WILL KILL HIM! YOU CAN'T DO THIS!
I COULD, BUT I THINK THIS TIME YOU WILL.
PICK UP THE LASH!
I AM ORDERING YOU TO PICK UP THAT LASH, MISTER!
DO YOUR DUTY. OR... I WILL DO MINE!
KARACK
SIR! THE TOPMAST YARD!
CAST THE LONGBOATS!

28

GO AFTER YOUR FRIEND!
HELP! SOMEONE-- HELP!
I'M HERE, MARY!
HAWKON! GET THE KEY! HURRY!
HAWKON--!

THANK GOD, YOU'VE COME, HAWKON!
WE'RE NOT OUT OF IT YET!
THE LEG IRONS!
HAWKON, HURRY!

RELEASE THAT LINE AT ONCE!
WE'RE WAITIN' FOR THE LAD AND LASS!
PULL HIM IN!
GET AWAY BEFORE SHE GOES UNDER!
31

GRAB THE LINE, JENS!
HAWKON--!

33

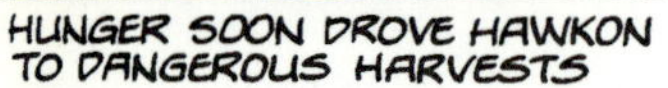
HUNGER SOON DROVE HAWKON
TO DANGEROUS HARVESTS

34

AHH...

JENS! MARY!
JENS...? MARY--? ANYBODY?
I WONDER WHAT'S UP IN THERE?
SOMEONE'S BEEN HERE!
YIPE!

36

HAWKON WAS DETERMINED TO DISCOVER THE DARK SECRET OF THE CAVE.

A TREASURE! I'M RICH!

UNLESS WHO HID IT HERE COMES BACK FOR IT!

WHAT'S THIS PAPER?

REWARD
£10,000
MERRICK
SCOURAGE OF THE SEVEN SEAS
WANTED DEAD OR ALIVE
IT'S MISTER HOWELL!

THIS MUST BE HIS TREASURE! HE'LL BE COMING BACK FOR IT!
THAT WAS HIS PLAN ALL ALONG!
I'VE GOT TO BE READY!

38

HAWKON MAKES A TRAP.

DINNER!

NOW IF I CAN JUST REMEMBER WHERE ALL THESE TRAPS ARE, MYSELF!

I THINK I'LL GO SEE WHAT'S ON THE OTHER SIDE OF THIS ISLAND OF MINE!

WHAT'S THAT?
IT'S ...THE FLORA!
MARY...

AH,
MARY...
JENS...

THERE'S
SMOKE ON
THAT OTHER
ISLAND!
SOMEONE'S
THERE!
JENS TOLD ME
HOW THE NATIVES
DID THIS, BUT HE
DIDN'T SAY HOW MUCH
WORK IT WAS!

MARY!
DON'T! LEAVE ME ALONE!

NO! NO!

AAAA!!!!!--!

HAWKON? HAWKON!
I KNEW YOU WERE ALIVE! I KNEW IT!

NO TIME FOR A REUNION! I'VE GOT TO GET YOU OUT OF HERE!
WAIT, HAWKON! YOU DON'T--

I HAVE A DUGOUT TIED TO A TREE NORTH OF HERE! RUN! I'LL FIGHT THEM OFF AS LONG AS I CAN...
HAWKON...

MOVE, MARY! I DON'T KNOW HOW LONG I CAN KEEP THEM BACK.
WHAT ARE YOU GONNA DO, KID, TAKE ON THE WHOLE VILLAGE BY YOURSELF?

JENS!
COME ON, JENS, WE CAN TAKE THEM--!
SURE, WE COULD...THEY'RE PEACEFUL AND FRIENDLY. THEY SAVED OUR LIVES!
HUH?

BUT MARY WAS FIGHTING THEM!
OH, THOSE BOYS? THEY CLAIMED ME AS THEIR SISTER AND NOW THEY WANT ME TO CLEAN UP AFTER THEM! THEY CAN FORGET IT!
SHE FIGHTS WITH THEM EVERY NIGHT!

WHAT ARE THEY SAYING?
THEY SAY YOU MADE A HELL OF AN ENTRANCE!

THEY PULLED US FROM THE SEA.
SINCE THEN WE'VE BEEN TRAVELLING FROM ISLAND TO ISLAND LOOKING FOR YOU...
...AND OUR MATES.

HOWELL'S REAL NAME IS MERRICK! HE'S A PIRATE!
AND I'VE FOUND HIS TREASURE!
I KNEW THERE WAS SOMETHING WRONG WITH HOWELL!

YOU REALLY FOUND A GENUINE PIRATE'S TREASURE?
HOW DO YOU THINK I GOT THESE?

IT'S BEAUTIFUL!
THERE'S LOTS MORE! I'LL SHARE IT WITH BOTH OF YOU! WE'LL GO BACK TOMORROW.

I'LL--UM--GO TELL THE CHIEF WE'RE LEAVING, AND --UH--THANK HIM.

44

TWO DAYS. WE'LL BE BACK IN TWO DAYS.
LET'S GO!

SO I MADE THIS HOLLOW TREE INTO A KIND OF SECRET HOUSE!
AND MADE TRAPS FOR MERRICK, TOO! GOOD LAD!

WATCH IT! THAT'S ONE OF MY TRAPS RIGHT THERE!
YOU'RE GOOD, LAD-- I DIDN'T SEE IT!

IF ANY PIRATES LEFT TREASURE HERE, THEY'LL COME BACK FOR IT, SOME DAY.
WELL, THIS TREASURE IS MINE NOW!
A MAN HAS TO PROTECT WHAT'S HIS!

I'M IMPRESSED, HAWKON--YOU'VE PUT TOGETHER QUITE A PLACE HERE.
IT'S A REAL XANADU, FIT FOR A KING.
I'VE FELT A LITTLE LIKE A KING HERE... BUT IT ISN'T LIKE HOME.

FIRST WE'LL GO TO THE WRECK OF THE FLORA, TO SEE WHAT ELSE WE CAN FIND.
LATER I'LL SHOW YOU WHERE I'VE HIDDEN THE TREASURE.
LOOK! A SHIP! WE'RE RESCUED!

IT'S A PIRATE SHIP!

IT'S HOWELL!
YOU MEAN MERRICK! HE HAS COME BACK FOR HIS TREASURE!
THEY'RE HEADED RIGHT FOR ONE OF YOUR TRAPS!
NO ONE STEALS FROM JOHN MERRICK AND LIVES TO TOAST A DRINK TO IT!
BLAST! MY TRAP DIDN'T WORK! HE GRABBED THE WRONG VINE!
MY TREASURE IS GONE!
THE MARKS ARE FRESH! WHOEVER TOOK IT IS STILL HERE! I WANT MY TREASURE FOUND!
I WANT EVERY ROCK, EVERY TREE, EVERY HOLE IN THIS CURSED ISLAND SEARCHED! NOW!

WHEN WE FIND THEM, WE'LL BURY THE WRETCHES UP TO THEIR NOSES IN THE SAND-- AND LET THEM WATCH THE TIDE COME IN!
NO! BETTER YET! WE'LL BURY THEM UP TO THEIR NECKS-- THEN WE CAN HEAR THEM SCREAM!

WORK... WORK...

GO BACK TO THE SHIP AND GET THE REST OF THE MEN. WE'RE GOING TO NEED THEM.
AYE, AYE, CAP'N. I'LL JUST LEAVE A COUPLE AS GUARDS.

HAVE A COUPLE OF THEM SLAVES BRING AN EXTRA BOAT OF SUPPLIES. WE'LL BE SPENDING THE NIGHT HERE.
THE REST OF THEM I WANT LOCKED UP!
AYE, SIR.

47

COME! WE'LL LOOK IN THIS DIRECTION!

THEY'VE GONE AWAY!
WE'LL WAIT UNTIL DARK, THEN SLIP OFF THE ISLAND WITH THE TREASURE!

SHOVE OFF!

LOOK! IN THE SECOND BOAT! IT'S BERG AND STEIN! THEY ARE ALIVE!
MAYBE THAT MEANS THE OTHERS ARE, TOO!

I RECALL A TIME OFF TORTUGA...
YOU'VE TOLD US THAT ONE A HUNDRED TIMES!

WE'RE NOT LEAVING WITHOUT THEM!
COME ON, I'VE GOT AN IDEA!

...YOU'RE BOTH WRONG! I'M THE ONE WHO SHOULD SNEAK PAST THE SHIP'S WATCHMEN!
NO! IT'S TOO DANGEROUS!

WHY? BECAUSE I'M A GIRL? I SNUCK ABOARD THE FLORA WHEN YOU WERE ON GUARD, DIDN'T I?
I'LL GET PAST THOSE PIRATES BETTER THAN YOU EVER COULD!
I BELIEVE HER.

WELL, ALL RIGHT.
BUT BE CAREFUL.
WAIT FOR OUR SIGNAL, THEN CARRY OUT THE PLAN.

BUT WHAT IF YOU'RE CAPTURED--?
THAT ISN'T GOING TO HAPPEN...
...BUT IF IT DOES, YOU SAIL AWAY WITHOUT US. TAKE MY SHARE OF THE TREASURE TO MY FAMILY.

GIMME!

BY SUNRISE ALL THE PIRATES WERE ASLEEP.

BAUMM
POW
50

BLAM PA-LAM
KA-BLAM
WE'RE UNDER ATTACK!
OVER HERE! THEY'RE OVER HERE!
GIT 'EM!
BLAM
KONK
UNK--!
THIS WAY!
SOME PARTY, HUH, MATES?

WE THOUGHT THE TWO OF YOU WERE DEAD FOR SURE!
AND THE LASS?
SAFE.
WE HOPE...

WHERE... ARE...WE... RUNNING... TO?
A DUGOUT CANOE...THEN TO THE SHIP!
WITH ANY LUCK, MARY'S ON BOARD...AND HAS RELEASED OUR MATES! QUICK! HIDE!

WHERE ARE THOSE SCUPPERS?

BLAM
THERE THEY ARE! OVER THERE!

COME ON, WE'RE TAKING A SHORT CUT!

THIS WAY! WE CAN SHOOT THEM FROM OVER THERE!

YOU GO ON AHEAD -- I'LL DIVERT THEM!
I'LL CATCH UP! NOW GO!
NO, JENS!

HEY, YOU LUBBERS! OVER HERE!

BLAM

WE'RE TRAPPED!

THIS IS MY ISLAND AND NO ONE TRAPS ME ON IT!

AMAZIN'!

I'LL WAIT FOR JENS.
YOU'RE CRAZY, LAD!

BLAM

WE GOT HIM!

AAIII--
WHAT THE--

ALL RIGHT, SWING IT BACK OVER!

JENS!
THIS WAY!

POW

LET'S HOPE...
...MARY HAS DEALT...
...WITH THOSE ON THE SHIP!

HMM, GUNFIRE...
WHAT BAD LUCK TO BE STUCK HERE, WITH ALL THE FUN BEING ASHORE.
MURPLE...

I'M A FIGHTIN' MAN, MIND YOU--SAILED WITH THE BEST!
HAW, MAYBE I SHOULD SAY, SAILED WITH THE WORST!
MUZZ WOPPLE?

AYE, TOO SLOW, MISS! I HEARD YE!

SAY YER PRAYERS, QUEENIE, 'CAUSE I'M GONNA GUT YA, WOMAN OR NO WOMAN!

NOW TO RELEASE OUR CREW, GET THE TREASURE ABOARD, AND GET READY TO SAIL!

I CONFESS, I NEVER THOUGHT IT WAS YOU, YOUNG HAWKONSEN.
NOW, WHERE...IS...MY TREASURE?

FIRST YOU'LL TELL WHERE IT IS, THEN I KILL YOU.
JUST REMEMBER, THERE ARE EASY WAYS TO DIE AND THERE ARE HARD WAYS TO DIE!

AH, ONE OF MY TRAPS!
DON'T STALL WITH ME, BOY!
MAYBE 1 SHOULD START BY KILLING YOUR FRIENDS, ONE BY ONE...SLOWLY!

MAYBE WE SHOULD START THE KILLING WITH JENS!

SHOOT HIM AND I'LL NEVER TELL YOU!
OH, I THINK YOU WILL, YOUNG HAWKONSEN!
MAYBE IF I JUST SHOT YOU IN, SAY, THE KNEE?
JUST ONE STEP MORE...
SHOOT ME AND YOU'LL NEVER FIND MY TREASURE!
YOUR TREASURE--?
TWANNG
AAARRRGH!
GET ME DOWN, YOU BLASTED FOOL!
UH-OH!

AFTER THEM!

YOU'RE NOT FINISHED WITH ME YET, BOY!
POW
BLAM

THEY'RE CATCHING UP!
OVER THE SIDE!

HURRY!

BLAM

HURRY,
PLEASE
HURRY!
THUNK
POW
FIRE!
BOOM
BAROOM
YOU
ALL RIGHT,
HAWKON?
GOOD
SHOOTING,
MATES!
YOU'RE NOT
FINISHED WITH
ME YET,
BOY!
59

ARRR--!

GRAB MY HAND, HAWKON!

DAMN YOU, BOY!

SET THE SAILS!

I'LL FIND YOU! IF I HAVE TO, I'LL SEARCH EVERY PORT IN THE WORLD!

60

AFTER THEM!

NO ONE STEALS JOHN MERRICK'S GOODS!

NO ONE! NO ONE!

SPRING IN NORWAY...
WHERE ARE WE GOING TO LIVE, MAMA?
WE HAVE RELATIVES WE CAN STAY WITH... FOR AWHILE.
THEN... THINGS WILL BE FINE.
PAPA! PAPA!

MAMA!
MAMA! IT'S ME, HAWKON!

I MISSED YOU, MAMA...I MISSED YOU!

THIS IS MARY SMITH. SHE'S GOING TO BE STAYING WITH US.

WHY ARE YOU PACKING UP?
I'M GLAD YOU'RE BACK, SON... BUT WE LOST THE FARM. IT'S TAKING A LONG TIME FOR MY LEG TO GET WELL.
WERNES LET US STAY THROUGH THE WINTER... BUT NOW...NOW WE MUST GO.

NO, WE DON'T!

I BOUGHT THE FARM THIS MORNING!
WHAAAT?

AND I HAVE PRESENTS FOR ALL OF YOU!
OH, YOU GOT ME ANOTHER!
AM I HOME NOW, HAWKON? REALLY HOME?
FOR AS LONG AS YOU WANT.
OLE, BRING THE BAGS IN.
YESSIR!
The End